Dear Parents and Educators,

Welcome to Penguin Young Readers! As par[...] know that each child develops at his or her [...] speech, critical thinking, and, of course, re[...] Readers recognizes this fact. As a result, ea[...] book is assigned a traditional easy-to-read lev[...] Guided Reading Level (A–P). Both of these systems will help you choose the right book for your child. Please refer to the back of each book for specific leveling information. Penguin Young Readers features esteemed authors and illustrators, stories about favorite characters, fascinating nonfiction, and more!

Guppy Up!

LEVEL **1**

GUIDED
READING
LEVEL **D**

This book is perfect for an **Emergent Reader** who:
- can read in a left-to-right and top-to-bottom progression;
- can recognize some beginning and ending letter sounds;
- can use picture clues to help tell the story; and
- can understand the basic plot and sequence of simple stories.

Here are some **activities** you can do during and after reading this book:
- Opposites: Opposites are words that express different concepts or ideas. The author uses many opposites in this book. For example, the words *up* and *down* are opposites. Reread the story and look for opposite pairs of words, such as *up* and *down*. Then write the words on a separate sheet of paper. Discuss the different meanings of the words.
- Rhyming Words: On a separate sheet of paper, make a list of all the rhyming words in this story. For example, *tail* rhymes with *nail*, so write those words next to each other.

Remember, sharing the love of reading with a child is the best gift you can give!

—Bonnie Bader, EdM
   Penguin Young Readers program

*Penguin Young Readers are leveled by independent reviewers applying the standards developed by Irene Fountas and Gay Su Pinnell in *Matching Books to Readers: Using Leveled Books in Guided Reading*, Heinemann, 1999.

For Jennifer, who always thought I could —JF

Penguin Young Readers
Published by the Penguin Group
Penguin Group (USA) Inc., 375 Hudson Street, New York, New York 10014, USA
Penguin Group (Canada), 90 Eglinton Avenue East, Suite 700, Toronto, Ontario M4P 2Y3, Canada
(a division of Pearson Penguin Canada Inc.)
Penguin Books Ltd., 80 Strand, London WC2R 0RL, England
Penguin Group Ireland, 25 St. Stephen's Green, Dublin 2, Ireland (a division of Penguin Books Ltd.)
Penguin Group (Australia), 250 Camberwell Road, Camberwell, Victoria 3124, Australia
(a division of Pearson Australia Group Pty. Ltd.)
Penguin Books India Pvt. Ltd., 11 Community Centre, Panchsheel Park, New Delhi—110 017, India
Penguin Group (NZ), 67 Apollo Drive, Rosedale, Auckland 0632, New Zealand
(a division of Pearson New Zealand Ltd.)
Penguin Books (South Africa) (Pty.) Ltd., 24 Sturdee Avenue, Rosebank,
Johannesburg 2196, South Africa

Penguin Books Ltd., Registered Offices: 80 Strand, London WC2R 0RL, England

Copyright © 2013 by Jonathan Fenske. All rights reserved. Published by Penguin Young Readers,
an imprint of Penguin Group (USA) Inc., 345 Hudson Street, New York, New York 10014.
Manufactured in China.

Library of Congress Cataloging-in-Publication Data is available.

ISBN 978-0-448-49646-7 (pbk) 10 9 8
ISBN 978-0-448-46331-5 (hc) 10 9 8 7 6 5 4 3 2 1

GUPPY UP!

by Jonathan Fenske

Penguin Young Readers
An Imprint of Penguin Group (USA) Inc.

Guppy up.

Guppy down.

Guppy smile.

Guppy frown.

Guppy gill.

Guppy tail.

Guppy hammer.

Guppy nail.

Guppy in.

Guppy out.

Guppy laugh!

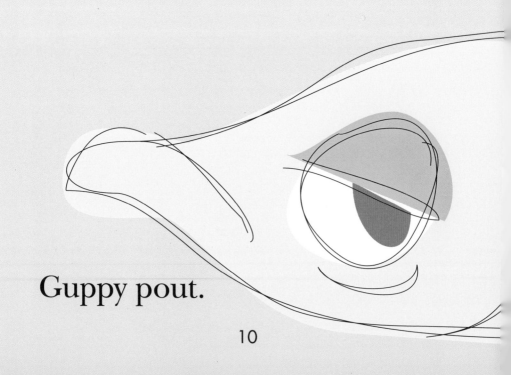

Guppy pout.

Guppy handle.

Guppy spout.

Guppy flops in the mud.

Guppy mops in the flood.

13

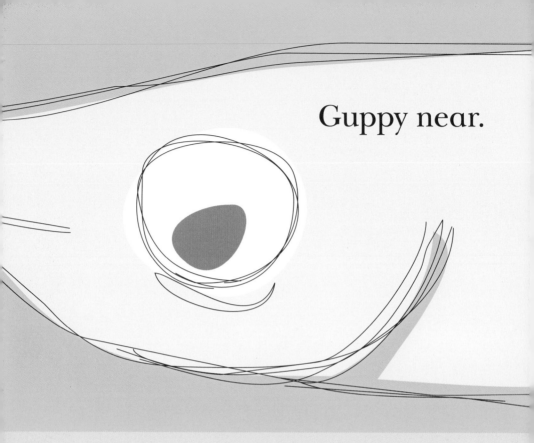

Guppy near.

Guppy far.

Guppy strums a guitar.

Guppy winks.

Guppy thinks.

Guppy sinks

and sinks

and sinks.

Guppy sock.

Guppy shoe.

Guppy drum.

Guppy kazoo.

Guppy tip.

Guppy top.

Guppy chip.

Guppy chop.

Guppy ship.

Guppy shop.

Guppy sips on a drink.

Guppy drips on a sink.

23

Guppy stop.

Guppy go.

24

Guppy fast.

Guppy slow.

Guppy house.

Guppy lawn.

Guppy bed.

Guppy yawn.

Guppy off.

Guppy on.

Guppy here.

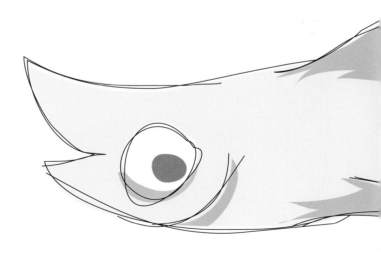